Do *YOU* See What I *SEE?*

Do *YOU* See What I *SEE?*

Brenda Wilson

ReadersMagnet, LLC

Do You See What I See?
Copyright © 2018 by Brenda Wilson

Published in the United States of America
ISBN Paperback: 978-1-948864-00-8
ISBN eBook: 978-1-948864-01-5

All rights reserved. No part of this publication may be reproduced, stored in a retrieval system or transmitted in any way by any means, electronic, mechanical, photocopy, recording or otherwise without the prior permission of the author except as provided by USA copyright law.

No lines, parts, and quotations were taken from other books or any previous publications.

The opinions expressed by the author are not necessarily those of ReadersMagnet, LLC.

ReadersMagnet, LLC
10620 Treena Street, Suite 230 | San Diego, California, 92131 USA
1.619.354.2643 | www.readersmagnet.com

Book design copyright © 2018 by ReadersMagnet, LLC. All rights reserved.
Cover design by Ericka Walker
Interior design by Shieldon Watson

CONTENTS

Prelude 7

Another Realm 9

A Dove of Peace 13

The Albino 17

Ellijay, Georgia 19

The Three Wise Men 23

The Wind Beneath His Wings 25

The Gaggle 27

Gertrude the Guinea 31

Long Term Commitment 37

The Scarlet Thread 39

Endnotes 47

PRELUDE

Who does not like to be in control or at least believe that they are in control. Most of us want it all, to control it all that is.

We plan the tomorrow, tonight, and planned tonight all day today. Sometimes I think we spend so much time planning that we almost forget to live. We certainly go on automatic pilot doing what we must do and never pausing to see the world around us.

It has been my experience that it is usually at a time when I think that I am most certainly in control that my Almighty Father in a fit of humor chooses the most unusual ways to show me just how little I pay attention and who really is the boss.

Traveling a unique stretch of highway either alone or in the company of my husband has taught me to live expecting the unusual at any given moment. Not only to expect something but to look for it and forward to it. To learn that to live life is a gift, to live it with peace and joy is a blessing.

If you are up to a short journey, continue to turn these pages and tell me "Do You See What I See?"

ANOTHER REALM

Sitting in the tinder, (a small boat that acts as a shuttle), slicing through the Gulf of Mexico to an area above Sweet Sugar Key, this land-locked lady marveled at what was taking place today.

Reaching forty and five, I was not so slim and trim as some of the younger ladies sitting next to me, but I was ready for this. My husband of twenty five years and I had taken and completed an open water diving course. This fulfilled a goal we had set as newly weds along with some others. We shared a desire to learn to dive and go cruising. Well, we were on our way.

Fresh water diving was an adventure in itself. To swim with fish in a large lake, feed them, note the visibility which always seemed a murky gray green, and realize that a whole different life went merrily about its business as we went unwittingly about ours was amazing.

Spray from the ocean waves brought me back to the moment. The warm tropical sun warmed my back. My heart fluttered with excitement as the small diving boat slowed and gently rocked us back and forth.

My husband at my side, we checked our gear, donned our fins and face mask and when cued by the crew, took the plunge.

The warmth of the tropical water was the first shock of the dive. This northern land lover had become accustomed to the shocking cold, fresh water at the beginning of a dive. This, however, was like an unexpected tepid bath.

Visibility was incredible, at thirty-five feet descent, I felt like I was looking across my living room. The exception was the brilliant colors and the unusual landscapes and unfamiliar critters to behold.

Gazing around me, I saw red, blue, green, and yellow sea fans waving as if to welcome me to their world. Taking in the landscape of the sea bottom, I saw brain coral resting by star fish in the sand. There was no mistaking brain coral as it was a dead ringer for the human brain.

Fish of all sizes and shapes swam about us and curiously pondered what species of fish we might be. It certainly seemed they did as they showed little fear and a great deal of interest.

Suddenly in front of us was a long fish with a trumpet-shaped mouth, eyes bulged out on either side. Although I could not hear one single note, only the rhythmic bubbling of my respirator, I believed I had just been serenaded by "Sachmo" better known as "Louie Armstrong" of the water world.

Pointing out some of the highlights, our master-diver directed our focus to a little sea horse. This little creature, almost translucent, attached itself to our caravan and traveled alongside us in this new world of wonder. Sea urchins studded the sand bottom beneath us. Crabs withdrew into crevices as we swam past.

Tiny little flashes of light caught my eye in first one place then another until my husband swam up alongside, and a little neon blue fish was attached and peeking in through his face mask as if to question, "Are you in there?" It was such a comforting tiny light in the darkness of the sea.

I saw pink squirrel fish, and golden parrot fish shining. Sergeant fish swam by in a school and had all of their stripes neatly in a row.

Clowning around was the clown fish who had his face painted as well as Emmett Kelly on any given day.

Moray the eel didn't give me a shock, but the octopus did that skittered over a rock. A stingray glided above me with his bite still in his tail. There was a frog fish with legs that never did hop. We looked on in amazement until the master diver signaled bottom time was up, and it was time for us to stop. I looked up at the sunlight streaming thirty-five feet down under and began swimming to the top.

I climbed the boats' ladder toward that very same sun and silently waved goodbye to my new sea friends. Plopping on the deck with a fishy wet sound, I marveled at the whole new world I had found.

A question arose as I thought about my day. I live on the earth with a whole different atmosphere down under. If men could walk on the moon, and there could be such separate worlds above the earth and below, did this not support the concept of a heavenly sphere? It served to show me the wonders that await we can't even imagine. We must prepare, take the leap of faith, and marvel at the world we see and what we believe to be.

A DOVE OF PEACE

Spring had arrived at the Wilson house as usual bringing with it a flurry of robins, starlings, sparrows, and this year some new visitors had joined the group.

We awoke daily to the call of turtle doves, cooing to the right, cooing to the left and cooing on every side of our house. My grandmother use to call them rain crows, and I still think of her when I hear their mournful call in the morning and in the evening.

Running the morning race as usual, I seemed far more irritable than usual for me. Not being sure why, I continued to hurry through my morning routine.

I had to shower, but we were out of hot water. I went to brush my teeth, we were out of toothpaste. I grabbed my freshly dried clothes from the dryer only to find that the wrath of wrinkles had attacked them while I was showering. A heel on the selected pair of shoes broke, and my hair took on a life of its own.

You get the picture.

On and on it went from one little wild fire to another.

The dog wouldn't come in the house after I had let him out. We were out of treats so I had to find something to substitute. I couldn't find my glasses. I couldn't find my car keys, and all the while the minute hand on the clock kept reminding me just how very late I was going to be.

Some mornings this would not have seemed like such a big deal, but today of all days I had meetings back to back, no wriggle room at all in my schedule, and no tolerance for anymore of this foolishness.

Once I had managed to throw on some mismatched outfit, plastered my hair down with hair spray, and slipped into an old beat up pair of shoes, I found my keys and headed for the door.

I drug myself into the car and turned to key. Thank heavens the car started. I remembered to raise the garage door and backed the car out.

Finally, I was on my way. I grabbed the cell phone out of my purse and hit the speed dial for work. It didn't ring. I hesitated long enough to look down and see that the phone battery was run down.

"Well great! Just great!" I mumbled and grumbled under my breath. I went to pull away from a stop sign and almost caused an accident in not seeing the car coming through the intersection through my fury.

No longer mumbling, I growled out loud about how ridiculous the morning had been. It wasn't fair! The faster I tried to go the slower my progress seemed.

Most times I could will the bad karma or whatever was causing my distress away. I could just push through the mayhem and gain control of my life, or so I thought.

Starting down the highway, I saw the road construction sign ahead. Several cars ahead of me were slowing to a caterpillar's crawl, and soon we would all be stopped. Wonderful, just wonderful. I stepped hard on the break pedal as I rolled my windows down to get some deep breaths of fresh air. This is supposed to help calm a person in those stressful situations. Much to my irritation all I heard was the intermittent calling of the doves. While glaring out the window on the driver side of my car and breathing deep, I was startled by the brilliance of a white bird floating down towards my windshield. Being so taken off guard by this creature, I watched as this beautiful bird I now recognized as a dove drifted over the hood of my car and rose to the branches of a maple tree in our yard.

I would catch a flicker of brilliant white as the branches of the tree swayed to and fro in a sudden cool gentle breeze. Now I had seen many a grey brown turtle dove, but never had I seen a pure white dove in the wild.

The insistent honk, honk, honking of the cars behind me, brought me back to the day at hand. With it came a saying I had read somewhere once upon a time, "Your failure to plan does not create a crisis for me today." Umm, I decided that message might just apply to me as I thought about the few moments of quiet during the storm of my self-induced stress.

Quietly I bowed my spiritual head and thanked my Heavenly Father for those few moments of quiet.

Moving the car forward, rejoicing in finally being underway, I continued to the office and prepared to reap the reward of my being unprepared.

Pulling into the drive way and putting my car in park, I quietly recalled the scripture, "Stand still, and know I am God." Now that had never been a favorite verse of mine since I didn't do standing still very well.

Running through the front door of the office, I breathlessly asked the receptionist, "Where did you put Mr. Jones?", my first appointment for the day.

"Oh, he called about thirty minutes ago and cancelled, said that his car wouldn't start, and he would rather reschedule. He asked me to have you call him, and he hoped that you would understand." The receptionist read her hand written note as I passed by her on my dash down the hall.

"Thanks, I'll call him later," I muttered.

Oh how well I understood! "Thank you, Lord," I prayed over and over. He knew my circumstance before me. My failure to prepare had not created a crisis for Him. If I had just stood still and realized that it was not me, but God that was in control my day, I would have spared myself a lot of muss, fuss, and worry. I could have rejoiced as the rain crows called down the showers of blessings.

THE ALBINO

It wouldn't be long now. I just needed to tie up a few loose ends and head home, pack my bag and my husband and I would head out to meet our daughter and her family for an early Christmas in the mountains of Georgia. Such Fun!!! I could hardly wait. It had been almost seven months since we had seen our granddaughters, and this Nana needed a grandbaby fix.

Putting the finishing touches to the last two reports pending, I locked my files, grabbed my bag, and headed out the door.

It was customary for me to work late and to be finishing up on the high side of midnight did not bother me.

Heading down the road with a soft melody on the radio, I began mentally packing my bag for the trip.

It usually took about thirty or forty minutes to get from the office to my house. Living in the rural part of Missouri offered velvet black skies sprinkled with millions of stars to wonder about as I drove at night. Not something you could easily see in the city.

Cruising along after the long day, I found myself far too relaxed. Although the drive was not long, the quiet of the night and hum of the highway caused my eyelids to droop longer then was safe.

"Ooops!" There was someone's white horse outside the pasture fence. Now to see a cow out was not such a big deal, but you didn't often see a horse out.

This little break in the drive served to wake me up just a little. I paid close attention to the animal as I drove up along side the creature.

"Hey! What in the world?" Up came a short, bushy, white tail, Two ears akin to a mules rotated outward, an over the fence the ghostly animal went. It cleared the fence as if it had taken a dead run from the other side of the road. Now I know there are no Lipinstein's in the area, those beautiful white horses that can jump straight up in the air. That was a deer, an albino deer. I was amazed to have seen such a rare beauty in this still dark night.

Well, I wasn't sleepy any longer! That was awesome, absolutely great.

I drove on home with a song on my lips and joy in my heart at being shown such a wonder of God.

We packed our suitcases and off we went to see the grandchildren. The destination was a cabin in Ellijay, Georgia, somewhere on Margarita Mountain. I napped as my husband drove. Cat naps and long stretches of wakeful conversation passed the hours of the day and most of the evening.

ELLIJAY, GEORGIA

When we left Missouri on our way to Margarita Mountain, we knew it would be about thirteen hours including a few pit stops.

Humming down the highway with the expectation of seeing our two granddaughters sooner than later kept us alert and talking a good share of the time.

I took the opportunity to share with my captive husband the surprising event of the night or early morning before.

"Is there such a thing as an albino deer?" I quietly asked my husband who was focused on the road and the long trip ahead.

"What?"

"Is there such a thing as an albino deer?" I carefully posed the question again.

"Yeah, there is, but they're pretty rare." My once hunter husband replied. Then he asked, "Why?"

"Well, I think I saw one on the way home this morning." I gladly shared.

"H-m-m-m-m." Not exactly the response I had hoped for.

We continued on our journey and talked no more of albino deer.

Before long we were at the base of a mountain with a fork in the highway. It was the typical type of fork, one path leading to the left, and the other leading to the right. There was not a sign in sight to indicate which way to Ellijay or if this was the eagerly sought, Margarita Mountain.

My husband pulled into a little convenience store. While I stretched my legs, he went in and asked the clerk for directions. When he came out I asked, "Which way are we supposed to go?"

"Up the mountain." My husband answered matter of factly.

"What?" I abruptly responded since he had not indicated that we should go left or right.

"That's what the man said. I asked him which way to Ellijay. He raised his head and said, "Ya gotta go up the mountain. There you have it." my husband recanted. It is the type of response that made this woman understand why men hesitate to ask for directions.

Back in the car, we picked the road veering off to the left and started to climb what felt like a mountain. In the now pitch-dark night, it was a little tough to tell just exactly where we were.

My cell-phone jingled loudly scaring the sleepy out of me.

"Hello?" I answered

"Hey where are you guys?" my son-in-law's familiar voice quarried.

"We are going up the mountain!", take comma out I replied, in a flip tone. I told him our situation and which path we had chosen. The humor in his voice was lost on me. He began giving more detailed directions and assured me that we were on the right road and he would come lead us to the cabin once we reached the grocery store in Ellijay.

"Hey! What was that!?" I shouted, catching just a glimpse of something darting across the road. *What in the world do they grow on this mountain?* I watched as a huge lizard-like tail disappeared into the brush.

"Are you alright? My son-in-law called from my cell phone.

"Yeah! Just give me the directions, and we'll see you in a little bit," I answered hurrying to finish the conversation.

"What was that thing?" I asked my husband as I tried to recreate the image in my mind.

"I don't know. It was moving too fast to see." He answered. "What did you think it was?"

I closed my eyes and relaxed. "Do you remember the movie Jurasic Park?" I asked.

"Yes.", came a single word response.

"Do you remember the Raptors that moved like lightning and ran in herds?"

My husband slowly turned his head my direction and looked at me as if I had grown a tail.

"Look I know it wasn't a Raptor, but the profile was really similar…it was a Kangaroo!!!" I yelled. "I know it was a kangaroo!"

This time he looked at me like I'd grown three heads as well.

"I don't know. That's just what it looked like to me." I ended the conversation.

Finally, we saw the little grocery store that was to be the meeting place under the only "Welcome to Ellijay Georgia", sign we had seen. I called our son-in-law, and in a few minutes we were climbing the last bit of distance to the cabin.

Greetings from the granddaughters and our daughter made the trip worth it all. We helped get the girls to bed and then gathered around a fire in the fireplace for some grown-up conversation time.

Our son-in-law's parents were at the cabin as well, and the plan was to celebrate an early Christmas in the Georgia part of the Smokey Mountains.

"S-o-o, I hear you saw a kangaroo, Brenda," my son-in-law's father started in.

"I'm not sure what it was, but it was really moving." I tried to end it there.

No such luck. My son-in-law offered up that it might have been a turkey. Now I don't hunt, but living in Missouri, I know that turkeys roost at dark and I've never seen a turkey move like that.

"Maybe it was a coyote," my son-in-law's father offered.

"No. I've seen enough coyote in the wild to know it wasn't a coyote or a timber wolf," I answered hoping the wolf part would give pause to the issue.

The conversation turned to what we were planning on having for lunch the next day. Turkey is always good when you are thinking about celebrating Thanksgiving and Christmas together. Homemade noodles were added to the menu along with all of the traditional stuff.

Morning came soon and with it a dip in the hot tub on the deck for me and the little girls. We got out and dried off, and I heard my name being called.

"Brenda, what are you doing? Come on up here a minute." My husband called.

"Let me put my clothes on first." I called back.

"Just hurry on up here." He replied.

What could be so urgent? I hurriedly pulled some dry clothes on and dashed up the steps calling back to the girls that I'd be back shortly.

Arriving at the head of the stairs, looking at the living room area, I saw three very serious-faced men sitting on a couch.

"What's up?" I asked wondering if someone was in need of my nursing skill.

"Come here and sit down," my husband directed me.

"What?" I really could not imagine what was going on.

"Tell me what it was you saw last night?" my husband asked.

Enough already!

"A turkey, alright? I saw a turkey." I declared.

"No, really what did you see?" He prodded.

"I thought I saw a kangaroo. Now can I go back down to the girls?" I asked growing weary of this taunting.

"Just a minute. We have been sitting here looking at this journal of interesting things to do in and near Ellijay. They have an animal reserve close by that has the largest population of kangaroo outside of Australia." My husband handed me the journal with pictures of kangaroos no less.

"The one I saw last night was headed home, that's for sure!" I started back down stairs to the girls humming "Tis So Sweet to Trust In Jesus," smiling all the way. Maybe it really was an albino deer.

THE THREE WISE MEN

We returned to Missouri and back to work. My daily routine consisted of a thirty minute drive one way on highway 136 to get to work.

Time continued to race along after the adventure in Ellijay and we approaching the Christmas season for real.

On one cold morning driving down 136 and thinking of what Christmas was about and how good God had been to me and my family over the years, I caught an unusual image on a far hill.

I continued driving and slowed down enough to be able to really see exactly what was over the next hill.

Slowing the old woman, Mustang, I drove. I saw a single-humped camel standing in the middle of a farmer's field in Missouri. Now that was almost as unbelievable as the kangaroo. Much to my amazement there was not one but three camels.

What a wonderful way to celebrate the holidays! I looked for the camels each morning for the next few weeks and was always greeted with the reaffirming sight.

At the office we were making preparation for our Christmas luncheon, and during the conversation, I began telling of what I believed to have been a white dear. One of the workers who lived close to the area heard me and said. "Oh yes, there have been several sightings of an albino deer in the area."

I couldn't wait to get home and tell my husband.

Prompted by my white dear revelation, I began telling the story of the kangaroo in Ellijay. I then proceed to tell my co-workers that I had been watching three camels outside of town in some farmer's field for the past few weeks. One of the my co-workers spoke up and said, "I am so glad to hear you say that! I almost wrecked my car the other day when I saw what I thought was a camel in my rearview mirror.

That evening as I drove home, all three camels stood on the hill. I could not help but think of the Wise Men who looked with faith, saw what others missed, and had journeyed to see the Christ Child on camels, such an amazing creation of God.

THE WIND BENEATH HIS WINGS

On a very typical day during my trip to the office I had not yet reached Camel Hill on Highway 136. Humming a familiar song, I gazed off to my right as I cruised down the familiar road.

Wow! I was looking at the biggest bird I had ever seen! At least I thought it was a bird. No, maybe it was one of those ultra-light planes that people sometimes fly. Whatever it was tilted and headed straight for me. Strange, I have never seen an airplane of any kind that had its wings tipped up.

Coming closer, threatening to T-Bone me one layer up?, I realized that I was looking at a huge bird as it continued to soar my direction. I focused on the creature and realized that the feathers about the bird's head were pure white. I now understood that I was being granted a brief glimpse of our great nation's emblem in the wild. Mesmerized, I watched as the eagle soared effortlessly over the highway, over my car, and landing gently in the field to my left.

Such beauty, such grace, such power. I marveled at the wonder I was looking upon. My mind turned to a much greater force, the wind beneath the eagle's wings.

I continued to my office, parked my car in the lot, opened the door and stepped out. I hoped no one was watching, but I just had to see. I spread my arms wide, closed by eyes, and wondered what it would be like to glide effortlessly above the earth's surface on the breath of God.

THE GAGGLE

In years' past, I had discussed the nature of a gaggle of geese with my she-farmer friends at work. We spoke of how this term related to some children who ran in groups, some families which did everything as a clan and ducks. We always thought the term described ducks as well. There were fluffy white ducks, yellow ducks, mallard ducks, wood ducks, and ducks and ducks and ducks.

On a brilliant fall morning many years after the gaggle discussions, I was traveling down the well-known highway 136 on my way once more to the office. Marching toward me along the side of the left hand lane was not one, not two, not three, but seven coal-black ducks coming down the road single file.

Passing them in my car, I slowed and looked closely. Now I have seen white fluffy ducks, yellow ducks, mallard ducks, wood ducks, but never had I ever seen coal-black ducks, black ducks without one white, yellow or brown feather on them.

I grabbed my cell phone and called my ever-understanding husband. "What kind of ducks are solid black?" I questioned.

"Gosh! I don't know…wood Ducks are a dark brown." He answered.

"No. I mean black, like ebony. Just wondered," I said and closed my cell phone.

I went on to the office and thought no more about the little black soldiers marching down the road until I was on my way home later in the day.

Approaching the span of road where I had seen the ducks in the morning I looked to my right and then my left hoping to catch a glimpse of the little critters. They were no where to be seen and maybe never were.

Pushing my black mustang down the road as I hurried to work the next day, the very last thing I was thinking about was ducks. I reached the area where the ducks had been yesterday, and there they were. This time they were waddling down the right side of the road. The complete gaggle, bunch, flock, I wasn't sure what to call them, but there they were.

This day I mentioned the ducks to my co-workers. No one had seen solid black ducks, but one lady suggested that they might be coots. Coots! Now I had no idea what that was. I had heard of ole' coots and maybe had seen a few of those, but they were much taller and in no way resembled a duck.

I utilized the wonder of the web and found pictures of coots. They in fact were black in color, but the head was shaped different than what I had seen. Also, most coots had some white markings on them.

Still unsure of what these cute critters were, I began looking for the proper term for the bunch of them and wandered just what I was to glean in understanding from these black ducks.

Later that evening, a dear friend, who was fighting a losing battle with cancer, called and talked at length about her mortality. She lamented just how this parasitic disease was leeching the very life out of her. Always the fighter, she spoke of being so tired and finally understanding why people in her situation gave up. Once she had vented her distress, our conversation moved to lighter things, and I asked her about the odd black ducks.

"No, I can honestly say I've never seen black ducks," my friend laughed and being full of trivia educated me about what a group of ducks on the ground might be called. "Geese are gaggles. Birds are flocks. You have encountered a brace of black ducks." She laughed a deep, throaty belly laugh as I had heard her do so many other times.

Within the next few days my friend died with me at her side. It was only as I felt the black void of her absence in my life that I understood the ducks.

I remembered scripture that tells us to put on the full armor of God, and understood. The unusual black ducks were the color of my sorrow. The brace on both sides had me covered and would support me. The line of seven served to remind me of God's perfect number and the completeness of His plan. I knew even though I would miss my friend in the rest of this life, I would be fine and claimed the promise of eternity believing I would see my friend again as I found God's grace to be sufficient.

GERTRUDE THE GUINEA

It was a rare, really warm day in the summer. With all the talk about global warming, it seemed that summer in Missouri was growing shorter and cooler instead of warmer and longer.

My four year-old grandson was planning on coming to Nana's house and spending the afternoon. I was hoping to fill the kiddie swimming pool in our back yard, let the water warm up, and I could soak up some rays while the young energetic one took a little dip.

The pool had already been placed in our backyard, and I went to the back door to step out on our deck, turn the water on, and begin filling the pool.

Looking out my backdoor window, I saw a strange looking fowl running across the road from our neighboring sale barn into the lots just east of our house.

A peacock with no tail! Surely that would explain the fat oval-shaped body, the funny neck, and pointed beak. This bird waddled into the sunlight from the shadow of the wind break made of carefully placed evergreen trees.

No film, no working camera close, I grabbed my cell phone and started stalking this strange creature in my back yard. Try as I might, I could not get close enough to get a clear picture, not even with the zoom. I did manage to snap a decent outline of the bird's shape to verify that I had in fact seen this strange creature. A female peacock, that had to be what this was.

My grandson arrived, and my attention turned a different direction. When we went to the backyard to fill the pool and play until the water warmed a little, I could not keep from looking about for the now phantom bird.

After my daughter in law picked up my grandson and my husband came home, I shared with him the sighting of the early afternoon.

"Hmmm, I don't know what that would be." My now tolerant husband declared.

He had come to the conclusion that it was best just to agree because like the kangaroo of months past, the bird probably was around somewhere.

Several days passed. One evening upon arriving home, my husband sought me out in the kitchen. He just sort of hung around before finally asking me in a sheepish tone, "What did you say that bird you saw the other day looked like?"

"Oh, it had a fat oblong body, kind of like a peacock, but it didn't have a tail or a crown," I casually replied. "Got any ideas?"

"No, but when I went out to go to work this morning, I heard this funny cluck-a-ta-cluck-a-ta-cluck, so I started looking around. There was this weird looking bird in the lot north of the house making this continuous awful clucking. I asked around at work and someone thought it might be a guiney. I don't know what they look like either."

"Hmmmm, maybe you should search the net while I finish supper." I sounded very casual, but inside I savored the sweet knowledge that once more my strange sighting was real.

A few minutes later, my husband brought the computer to me and showed me an exact picture of the bird I had seen. It was in fact a guinea, I still did not know where it had come from or why it frequented our yard.

After sharing this new critter tale with the girls at work, one of them commented how good guineas were for watch dogs. She indicated that they functioned like an alarm anytime anything new or strange came into the yard. Recalling the noise my husband had described, I could see how that would be.

Several days later my husband shared with me that when leaving the house that morning, he had almost stepped on two young birds that he thought were fledgling doves. I had not noted anything coming home.

The next morning as I went to leave, I saw what he was speaking of, but instead of doves, they were two baby guineas. They were so near the color of dirt very quietly sitting there, that one could easily miss them. Guarding the front door, these two were learning from their mother who was nowhere to be seen, but certainly could be heard.

Arriving home after getting groceries, I proceeded to prepare our evening meal. My husband kept me company as did our old dog Mac. Mac seemed unusually occupied with the window in the kitchen. Watching him, my husband began telling me about the evening before I arrived.

He told of sitting in our downstairs living room with our old dog Mac. My husband was on his computer, and the television was on. Now since the house we live in has a complete living quarter upstairs and down, the windows downstairs are high on the walls.

Completely engrossed in his computer, my husband recanted hearing a strange tap, tap, tapping. Our dog began barking and running around. Before long the dog grew quiet and sat pensively by our downstairs door. I'd have liked to think this was in anticipation of me arriving home, but the story went on. Not long after the first occurrence, the strange tap, tap, tapping began again, and the dog went wild. Mac barked and ran around the down stairs having a difficult time locating the source of the strange noise. Once again true to the last time, the dog grew quiet and sat in anticipation at my husband's feet. Soon the tap, tap, tapping began for the third time. Looking up, my husband saw the recently acquired guinea pecking on the downstair's kitchen window. Upon Mac's loud defining of his territory, the strange bird pulled back, and all grew quiet eventually. The peace lasted until the brave guinea strutted to the window and began pecking one more time.

Upon reaching home, I found my husband laughing and my old dog looking quite bewildered.

I had great fun chiding my husband about the guinea come calling until several weeks later when my old dog Mac and I were dog-sitting the children's miniature dachshound. Sid is red in color, faster than greased lightening, and resembles the squirrels that plague Mac in our yard. Over time they have achieved a certain amount civility toward each other, most of the time anyway.

On this particular day, I was sitting downstairs with a cup of coffee, and Mac and Sid were sleeping on either side of my feet. Suddenly I heard a tap, tap, tapping on the window on the living room side of the downstairs. Mac immediately went into alert mode and began barking relentlessly. Sid had no clue what was going on, but thought perhaps she should help Mac out. She began running circles around him barking in synchronized rhythm to Mac's vocalization. What a ruckus!!! I glanced at the window just in time to see the strange head and scrawny neck of the guinea as she cocked her head to one side, peering into the living room intently, then promptly pecked on the window several times. This brought about a whole new onslaught of barking and running around. I watched as the guinea taunted the dogs or asked them to come and play, or to let her in. Whatever, there was no question that she wanted our attention.

I went about fixing a special supper of crow pie and sheepishly ate my portion when my husband got home, and I recanted the story for him.

Time passed and autumn turned to winter. It became bitter cold with snow and ice as often happens in Missouri. We didn't see the guinea or her chicks for several weeks, but we would occasionally hear her when we left or returned to our house. I hoped for her sake she was in a warm place and well feed.

On one particularly cold gray morning, I whined as I went out into the bitter cold. I heard the guinea but didn't take the time to look for her. At the end of our street is a wooden fence that has three stairstep posts in it. Each post is a few inches taller then the one before it. Easing my car to a stop at the stop sign, I rolled my window down to be able to see until the defroster kicked in, and there she was. Cluck-a-clucking away, even in this freezing cold morning, she sat at the edge of our yard and loudly proclaimed any coming or going in our direction. She had adopted us and was a well placed sentinel. I continued on my way and thought about strange Gertrude.

She found us, asked for a place in our hearts, shared her seed, and gallantly stood guard over us, demanding our attention when necessary. There is another Sentinel that found me, knocked on the door of my heart, shares the seed of hope, guards me, and will not let me ignore the guiding of my Lord.

LONG TERM COMMITMENT

Time keeps creeping up on me. I look in the mirror and no longer see the sassy young woman that I feel in my heart. Crows have left their foot prints at the corner of my eyes, frowns left furrows in my brow, and smiles are permanently lined around my mouth. When I get down on my knees, I pop and crack like those packing bubbles when you squeeze them.

The time was right and a plan to downsize was born.

Now no matter how much I think I have something planned out, it never goes exactly the way I think I have it planned. Either I move too fast or I move too slow. I just can't seem to get the knack of rolling along with a greater plan.

Imagine, if you can, someone taking a two-story home containing two complete houses used by one family for twenty years. This one family raised two teenagers during those twenty years. Take that home and put it in one half of a regular house. That was the plan.

We had leased the two-house home, and our tenant was already occupying the upper half of the place. The single gentleman asked if we could locate someone to clean for him, and this we did. A local young woman who came highly recommended and could work around our tenant's schedule was hired and began the cleaning routine.

One early spring evening, my husband came home and shared an interesting story with me. Since we were in various stages of moving stuff out of the downstairs of the two-home house, living up the road in my mother's house, and renovating the little house we would live in, we occasionally found it necessary to retrieve something from the first house. My husband said that he had done exactly that when the tenant stepped out on the porch and quaried, "Do you know you have a guinea around here?"

My husband laughed and assured him that we were well aware of that and had been for the past year.

The tenant shared that the cleaning lady had been waiting for him to return which was unusual for her. She recanted to him. "I almost didn't get to clean for you today!"

"Why is that?" he asked.

"Well your turkey just about wouldn't let me on the porch!"

My husband and I both laughed until tears rolled down our cheeks. Poor Gertrude had been mistaken for a peacock with no tail, an unidentified fowl, and now a turkey.

All the while, Gertrude was still a guinea, one that had committed to guard our house. Strange how things change. We had moved, but Gertrude remained.

I realized so it is with God, my Father. I don't always recognize Him for what He is, sometimes I don't see Him at all for a while, but He stays. It is me that moves, and He is faithful to remain steadfast in His commitment to me until I return to Him. No matter how I percieve Him, He is still the same—He is my God.

THE SCARLET THREAD

It was late in the day, I was eager to get home from the office. I had stayed later than usual and got caught up in a conversation with a coworker about how I met my dear friend "Jesus Christ."

I was due to arrive at a church meeting at just this very moment, and here I was bailing into my car and rushing down the road like a wild woman.

I have never understood why I believe that a few moments of random rushing will make up for my unplanned delay in timing, but I do. Grabbing my cell phone and speed-dialing my husband, I focused on the road as I raced toward the meeting that was destined to already have started a full half-hour's drive away.

Ring! Ring! Ring! My party was away from the phone, out of range, or some such nonsense. The meeting would just have to start without me, and I would get there just as quickly as I could.

Setting my cruise control so as not to be blessed with a speeding ticket, I began recalling the conversation I had just left. It is amazing how comforting it can be to share how God's grace changed my life. Even when I have told it over and over again, to tell it one more time is a blessing.

I suddenly bolted out of my reminiscing as a car crawled through a four-way stop, crossed the highway in front of me, and made me stomp on my brakes to keep from broadsiding the elderly driver in the other vehicle.

Now that little incident would truly have caused me to miss my church meeting. I stepped gently on the accelerator and trembled just a little knowing full well what a bad accident that might have been.

I had begun thinking again of God's love when a bright flash of brilliant red rose out of the ditch on the passenger side of my little black Mustang. A beautiful male cardinal swooped to the front of my car and made a bee line right down the middle of my lane. He appeared to be leading me down the road but a much slower pace than I would have chosen. He seemed to believe he was the perfect red hood ornament for my black car. I sputtered and fumed but was not willing to overrun this out-of-place, beautiful red bird. Finally after several minutes, I settled back, drove at the bird's pace, and relaxed. Almost at that very minute, the beautiful bird veered to the left, and I journeyed on my way down the infamous highway 136 resigning myself to the fact that I would miss the meeting altogether.

I went back to recalling my last conversation, the near accident, and the unusual bird. I pulled into the parking lot of the church since all of God's children were still gathered. Stepping out of the car, I remembered the words of a dear pastor as I once tried to make sense of the Old and then the New Testament. "All you have to do is follow the scarlet thread."

Walking to the meeting room, I was met with minimal murmuring from just a few who were to be there. I was sure I had missed the whole meeting. Much to my surprise, there sat my husband and one other team member. They were waiting on the others to arrive as an unforeseen circumstance had detained them.

What a blessing. Not only had I gotten to share my testimony, miss a wreck, see an out-of-place beautiful creation behaving strangely, but I had made it to my church meeting on time.

Finally, it dawned on me. Perhaps that is what happens when one just relaxes, lets go, and follows the scarlet thread to the cross.

One day a friend sent me this paragrph and pictures on e-mail. I am not sure of the name of the paper in France that published these or the unknown photographer was, but it touched me as I know it will you.

His mate is injured; she was hit by a car as she swooped low across the road.

He brought her food and attended to her with love and compassion.

He brought her food again, but was shocked this time to find her dead. Then he tried to move her (a rarely-seen effort for swallows).

Aware that his sweetheart is dead and will never come back to him again, he cries out with adoring love.

He stood beside her, telling the world that he is saddened by her death.

Do You See What I See?

Finally aware that she would never return to him, he stood beside her body with only sadness and sorrow.

> **Millions of people in America, Europe and India cried after seeing these photos.**
>
> **The photographer sold these pictures for a nominal fee to the most famous newspaper in France.**
>
> **All copies of that edition were sold out on the day these pictures were published.**
>
> **You have just witnessed Love and Sorrow Felt by God's creatures.**
>
> **And many people will still believe animals don't have a brain or feelings…**

The following words of wisdom have been to have been created by some unknown author, others believe them to be credited to, Upanishads, the most ancient Hindu Scripture. There are others who credit the Jewish Talmud for the following bitsof wisdom. I only know that such wisdom proves true over and over in my own life.

> **Watch your thoughts, for they become words;**
>
> **Watch your words, for they become actions;**
>
> **Watch your actions, for they become character;**
>
> **Watch your character, for it becomes destiny.**

The e-mail continue:

> Some would discount the photos as only animal instinct: Others would doubt the authenticity of the bird's apparent

feeling. Others might need to know who created such words of wisdom but if you look aound you, you will see it does not matter.

A world with out emotions of love, compassion, joy, sadness, yes even sorrow would be a bleak world in deed. Dare to look around and see what you could dare to believe.

ENDNOTES

1. Randy Faulk, Love For Our Birds, "Creatures Have Feelings, Even Swallows." Accessed November 30, 2012. http;//www,stair-assoc,com/birds_feelings_loyalty_devotion_honor_emotions_column.html.

2. Ibid

3. Think Exist.com, "Quotes about Actions." Last modified 2012. Accessed November 30, 2012. http://thinkexist.com/quotation/watch_your_thoughts-they_become_your_words-watch/13673.html.

www.ingramcontent.com/pod-product-compliance
Lightning Source LLC
LaVergne TN
LVHW020445080526
838202LV00055B/5340